Mary Malloy
·—· and ·—·
The Baby Who Wouldn't Sleep

For all the babies
I have rocked to sleep.

~ND~

First published in Great Britain 1993
by William Heinemann Ltd
an imprint of Reed Consumer Books Ltd
Michelin House, 81 Fulham Road, London SW3 6RB
and Auckland, Melbourne, Singapore and Toronto
Text and illustrations copyright © Niki Daly 1993
ISBN 434 96226 0
Produced by Mandarin
Printed and bound in Hong Kong

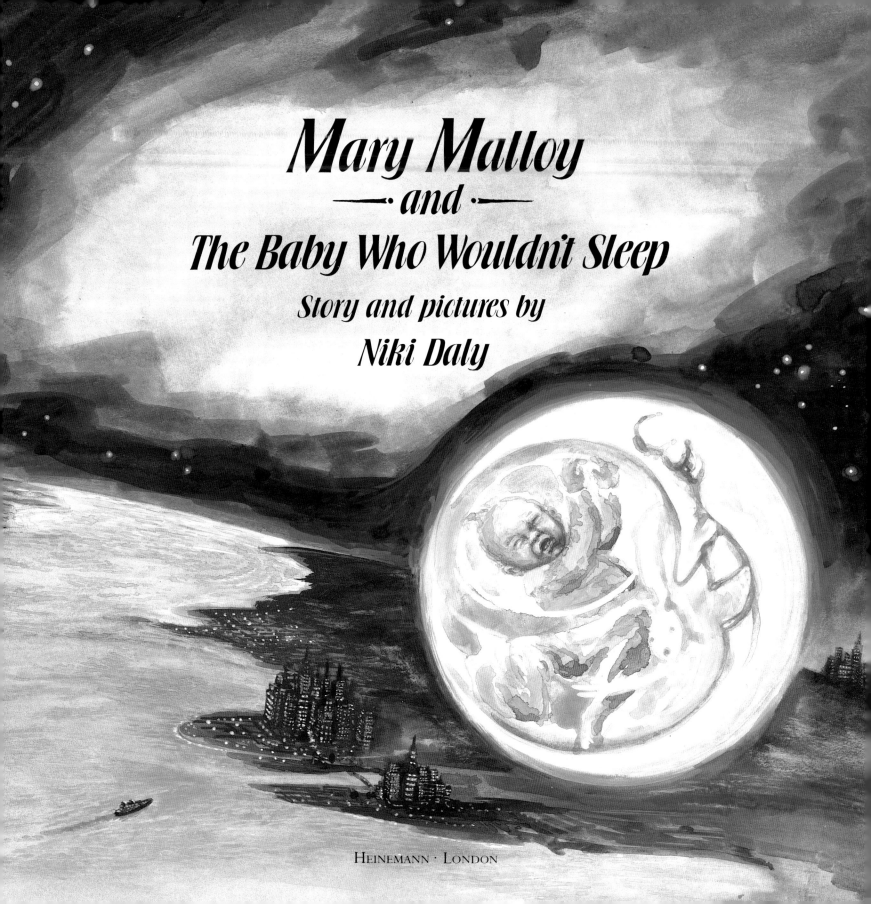

Mary Malloy
·— and —·
The Baby Who Wouldn't Sleep

Story and pictures by

Niki Daly

HEINEMANN · LONDON

Baby wouldn't go to sleep.

He cried, he hollered, he sobbed, he wailed.
He shook Mary Malloy right out of a dream.

Mary Malloy put on her hat and went to see Baby.
"What's wrong? Want a song?" whispered Mary.
"Boo-hoo-hoo!" cried Baby.

Mary Malloy carried Baby onto the verandah
where the cool evening air stroked Baby's hot cheeks.

"Go to sleep my Mama's cuckoo-lulu," sang Mary.
"Big Bear's gonna eat you up if you don't!"

Baby hullabalooed until the Crescent Moon
pushed aside her cloudy curtains and
smiled mysteriously down at Mary Malloy
and the baby who wouldn't go to sleep.

"Babies love being rocked," cooed Moon. "Let me rock him."
"Only if you're very careful not to let him fall," said Mary Malloy,
placing Baby into Moon's waiting arms.

"Oooh," crooned Moon, as Baby curled into her.
"I *do* love babies."

Full and round, Moon rocked Baby.
But Baby om-pom-pushed and boo-hooed
fit to wake the world.
"Moon," called out Mary Malloy,
"please don't hold Baby so tightly."
"Fiddle-sticks!" chuckled the moon.

"Moon, give me back Baby!" demanded Mary Malloy.
"Tricked you!" laughed the wicked moon from
behind her spidery curtains.

Now Moon tried to soothe Baby.
She hush-a-byed and kootchie-cooed.
She sang velvety lullabies across the Silver Sea.

"MOON! YOU THIEF,
BRING BACK BABY!"
Mary Malloy's voice echoed,
from the West to the East,
across the sea and over
cities that never sleep,
all the way to the distant Nile.

Moon! You thief,

There,
Mr Fez, the crocodile,
saw the moon above the Nile.
Caught its wicked moonlight smile
laughing on the water.

So this is what he did.

"Moon," called Mr Fez, "see what I have for you."
Moon looked down and eyed a beautiful water baby shining in the water.
"Aaah," sighed Moon, "I *do* love babies. And two are better than one!"
Moon beamed over the water. The water baby grew big and bonny
as Moon dipped and danced closer and closer.

Foolishly, Moon opened her arms to snatch up
the water baby and as she did so – *splash!* –
Baby fell into the bubbly Nile, right into Mr Fez's fishing net.
"Goo-goo," gurgled Baby – he had stopped crying.

"Tricked you, Moon!" laughed Mr Fez.
Quickly, he fished Baby out of the warm water.

Mr Fez placed Baby safely into his felucca,
and they floated bubbly, bubbly, down the Nile.

across the Silver Sea,

and before they reached journey's end,
where all friends meet, Baby fell fast asleep.

"Thank you and goodnight," whispered Mary Malloy,
carrying Baby back to bed.

High above, the Crescent Moon hung thin and sullen.
A tear fell from her eye and turned into an evening star.
Moon smiled sadly and sighed, "At least I have you."

Mr Fez gazed up at the sky and tenderly sang,
"Twinkle, twinkle, star so bright,
Shining in the pale moonlight."

"Kiss the Baby, cheek and chin.
Bless the bed that I lie in.

North, South, East, West
Choose the dream that you love best."

Goodnight!